Stop!
Before you turn the page —
Take a piece of paper.
Pick up your pencil.
Draw a big triangle.

At the top point of the triangle write **Secret Government UFO Test Base.** At the left point write **Dinosaur Graveyard.** At the right point, **Humongous Horror Movie Studios.** And in the exact center of the triangle write Grover's Mill.

Ah, Grover's Mill. A perfectly normal town, bustling with shops, gas stations, motels, restaurants, and schools. A small town with a great big heart, nestled snugly in the midst of —

Wait! Did we say normal? A studio where they film the cheapest horror movies ever made? The world's largest and smelliest graveyard of ancient dinosaur bones? A secret army base filled with captured alien spacecraft?

All this makes poor Grover's Mill the exact center of supreme intergalactic weirdness!

Turn the page.
If you dare.
r The Weird Zone!

THE INCREDIBLE SHRINKING KID!

THE WEIRD ZONE

THE INCREDIBLE
SHRINKING
KID!

by Tony Abbott

Cover illustration by Broeck Steadman
Illustrated by Lori Savastano

A
LITTLE APPLE
PAPERBACK

SCHOLASTIC INC.
New York Toronto London Auckland Sydney

ISBN 0-590-67434-X

12 11 10 9 8 7 6 5 4   6 7 8 9/9 0 1/0

Printed in the U.S.A   40

First Scholastic printing, July 1996

To the kids of
Middlebrook School

Contents

THE INCREDIBLE SHRINKING KID!

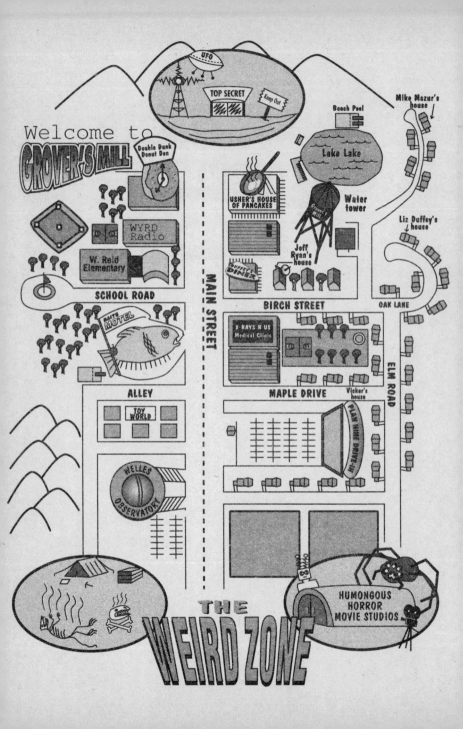

Sean Vickers pumped his spiffy blue and white bike up the dirt road. "No!" he cried. "They're too close!"

Sweat dripped from his forehead. He shook it away. He was out of breath. It was getting dark. He was hungry. He had to stop.

He couldn't stop!

The crunching, grinding sounds closed in on him fast. Faster! Faster!

"Gotta keep going!" he told himself.

Soon he would be on a bluff overlooking the town of Grover's Mill.

"I hope I make it!" he grunted. He started pumping uphill faster.

Clouds passed over a full moon, and a breeze swirled up behind him, sending a chill down his clammy back. Yuck!

Still, Sean pushed on, standing on the pedals and pumping hard over the gravel and dirt of the road. And still the sounds got closer.

They were following him!

Suddenly, his front tire twisted in the soft dirt. He drove his right foot down hard on the pedal.

No good! He lost time. He heard the horrible cry —

"Hey, floodpants! Wait up!"

Sean decided not to struggle. He gave in. He coasted to a stop.

Tires rolled up next to his. Attached to the tires were bikes and sitting on the bikes were his best friend, Jeff Ryan, and his not-so-best sister, Holly.

"Aren't you cold?" asked Holly, kicking at his pants with her foot.

Sean made an ugly face at her. But it was true about his pants. He'd shot up since the beginning of the year. It was now midsummer and he was growing out of all of his clothes. He looked like a scarecrow. He towered at least four whole inches over Holly.

"I stand tall," he proclaimed, posing like a comic book hero.

Sean and Jeff laughed together, posing like two muscular superheroes.

Holly pretended she was going to be sick. Sean laughed harder. She was the reason he was biking so hard. She was a year younger, and the galaxy wasn't big enough for the both of them.

Sean rested with one foot on his bike pedal, the other on the gravel road. "Grover's Mill. Some place, huh?"

"From this far up, it seems pretty normal," said Jeff.

"Yeah, then you open your eyes," Sean said, brushing his wavy dark brown hair away from his forehead. "I mean, just look around! A secret army base up there. A dinosaur graveyard over there. My dad's horror movie studio over there. And us in the middle. This place is the exact center of total galactic weirdness!" He turned to Jeff. "After being at camp for two weeks, I see it all so clearly."

"I can't see anything clearly," said Holly. "It's getting dark. Let's go home."

"At camp we learned to love the dark," Sean said.

"Get real," Holly snorted.

"No, really. I learned survival techniques." Then Sean snickered to himself. "Well, mostly I learned songs."

Sean started once more up the dirt road to a low rise overlooking Lake Lake.

"So why didn't you stay at Camp Goofy?" his sister quipped, pedaling alongside.

"It's called Camp Smiley," said Sean, screwing up his face and thinking about swatting his sister. But he backed off and smiled instead. He couldn't help it. That's what the camp counselor said. Whenever he remembered Camp Smiley, he would smile.

And it was true. He was doing it!

All three bikers coasted on a flat stretch. Big hulking bulldozers and steamrollers were parked on both sides of the dirt road.

"The best part of camp was this new kid I met, Mike Mazur." Sean went on. "His family just moved into a new house at the end of this road. The tenth house, Mike told me. It's white."

"We're late for supper," Holly said. "Besides, we're not supposed to be up here. Remember what Mom said about the equipment. It's dangerous. We could get hurt."

"I scoff at danger," Sean snapped. "Superheroes always do. You can go home if you want to." He gestured back down the hill.

Shadows flickered in the moonlight, going in and out of the clouds. Black streaks slashed the road behind them. The breeze sweeping up from the lake was steadying into a wind.

Without anyone seeing it, night had fallen.

Holly said nothing. She rode along next to Jeff.

Sean suddenly tore off around the first bend, leaving the others behind him again. He counted houses. "Five — six — seven. It's coming up!"

He banked fast through the corner and pedaled harder into a little straight before the next turn. He could make out three houses just ahead of him. A white one was at the end.

"Eight — nine — tttttt — "

FLAAAAAASH!

A powerful blast of purple light exploded in Sean's face.

"Ahhhhhh!" he screamed.

Have a Blast!

The force blew Sean backward. He skidded across the gravel and slammed hard into the huge tire of a bulldozer.

"Ow!" he moaned. He suddenly ached all over. He felt as if his breath had been completely knocked out of him.

Jeff ran over. "Wow, what a tumble! Are you okay?"

Holly coasted up to him. "Get the training wheels. My brother forgot how to ride."

"Oh, man," Sean groaned, feeling the back of his head for tread marks. "Did you see that?" He pointed to the clearing ahead. "That huge light?"

Holly looked up. "That's called the

moon, Sean," she snapped. "Say it, M-O-O-N!"

"No, it was a big purple light," Sean snarled. He turned to Jeff. "You saw it."

Jeff looked down. "Well . . ."

"Oh, man!" Sean groaned again. He grabbed Jeff's hand and pulled himself to his feet. He dusted off his pants and his W. Reid Elementary T-shirt. "Come on, let's find Mike's house."

Jeff trotted over to the road, stood there for a second, then came back. "I just counted, Sean. There *is* no tenth house. There are only nine."

Sean counted, too. Jeff was right. There was no white house. Suddenly Sean felt jittery all over.

"I guess my big brother doesn't know his numbers," said Holly. "Maybe when we get back to school, you should drop back a grade, Sean. I heard Principal Bell talking about it anyway."

In the distance — *bong!* — the clock on top of the Double Dunk Donut Den chimed the hour. A moment later — *ssss!* The pan sitting atop Usher's House of Pancakes hissed the hour, too.

"It's getting late," said Sean. "We'd better go home." He rubbed the back of his head again, hopped on his bike, and pushed off down the hill.

The next morning was hot and sunny. Sean greeted his parents at the kitchen table and opened the refrigerator. A blob of brown oozy stuff slid off the top rack and onto his hand.

He licked it off. "Mmm, not bad."

"Do you think so?" asked his mother.

Next Sean shook the milk carton and raised it to his lips. Thick blue liquid poured down his chin. After that he reached into a bowl on the counter, grabbed two eyeballs, and popped them into his mouth at the same time.

"Crunchy," he mumbled, showing red teeth.

"Ho, ho!" cried Mr. Todd Vickers, the not-

at-all-famous movie director, producer, special effects person, camera person, and in fact the *only* person at Humongous Horror Movie Studios. "Daisy, you've done it again! Hideous movie props you can eat! Dear, you are wonderful!"

Mrs. Daisy Vickers blushed. "I try."

"This is a little disgusting," said Holly, dipping her spoon into her cereal.

No, this is the Vickers household. A home full of gunk and goop. Fake monster heads and hands. Eyeballs in little bowls. Crawling hands under the sofa. Green oozy brains in the hamper.

"Is this any way for a kid to grow up?" asked Holly.

"No," said Sean, "but it's a good way for a kid to throw up!"

Mr. Vickers beamed at his two children, got up from the table where he was making notes for a new movie, and did a little dance across the floor. On the way, he grabbed Mrs. Vickers and twirled her around.

"Dad!" snorted Holly. "Please don't be weird. Someone could be watching."

"Ah, sorry, little one." Mr. Vickers halted in mid-twirl, but, oh, Mrs. Vickers didn't! She kept spinning and hit the table, her arms flying. Then she slammed the oven door — *wham!*

She quickly recovered her balance, and sang, "Ta-da!"

"Children," said Mr. Vickers, "today I have to check on scenery being built for my next film spectacular. A big bald guy stomps a little town. I call it *The Amazing Colossal Bloody Fiend From Beyond the Third Realm of Venusian Fire Attacks the Tiny American City of Grover's Mill.*"

"Oh, darling," Mrs. Vickers beamed. "I just *adore* the bloody fiend part, but will that lovely title fit on the sign, dearest?"

"Hmm," he mused. "Perhaps you're right, sweet cheeks. Anyway, I've asked a toymaker to create a little model town for my fiend to crush. It's a tiny version of our fair Grover's Mill!"

"A toymaker?" said Holly. "A jolly toy-maker? Maybe he's like old Pagetto, in *Chiponnio, the Puppet Boy*. Short and chubby with white hair, clicking his heels, always singing."

"Or maybe," said Sean, hunching his shoulders and swooping down on his sister, "he's the creepy guy in *Terrible Toymaker of Terrorville*!"

Holly backed up and hit the wall. Sean smiled.

"To the toy shop!" exclaimed Mr. Vickers, and headed into the garage.

The Vickers piled into the family car and made the short drive to Main Street in the center of Grover's Mill. Mr. Vickers parked and pointed to a row of stores. "A left at Vader's Glove Store. The toy shop is in the alley right around the corner."

Sean took off, leaping giant steps ahead of everyone.

But when he got to the corner, he screeched to a stop, and stared.

UFO! Sort of

It looked like a dream a kid might have the night before his birthday.

The little shop in the alley twinkled all over with tiny colored lights. Toys were stacked up in the windows in neat little arrangements.

It looked like a kid's dream, all right.

Except for one thing. Filling up the doorway, towering over everything, was a man.

Nope, it wasn't Pagetto, the chubby little toymaker. No way.

This guy was thin. And very tall. His hair was black, inky black, except for a streak of silver-white that shot back from his forehead to behind his left ear. He wore really thick glasses. And his long nose had long hairs curling out.

But the weirdest part of all was that his face was crooked. It was tilted, as if the two halves of his face didn't go together.

"The little child," the man said suddenly. He stepped forward from the doorway.

Sean looked around. He was the only one in the alley. "Me?" Then he pulled himself up taller. He started thinking of some snappish big superhero words to say. None came to him.

The man stepped closer. "The little child . . ."

Sean shuddered and shrank back.

"And his family!" the man said, stopping just as Holly and her parents ran up next to Sean.

Suddenly, the man's crooked face smiled. Well, half of it did. "Welcome to Kruger's Toy World," he said. Then he bowed really low and swept his hands toward the door. "I am Kruger."

"Now there's a howdy for you!" Mr. Vickers exclaimed.

"I'm going to order a pizza," said Mrs. Vickers. She swished across the street to Duffey's Diner as the others walked into the store.

"This is awesome," said Sean, staring at shelf upon shelf of all the latest toys advertised on TV. "He's even got Moto-Men! My favorites!"

Sean ran across the room to where dozens of mega-warrior Moto-Men stood shoulder to shoulder on a shelf. Each Moto-Man was ten inches tall with a face that was all rivets and blinking lights. The arms were rocket launchers.

Sean reached for one. Suddenly, the robot's little head turned to face him. "Exterminate!" droned a little voice. Then it shot its arm rocket.

Flonk! It bounced off Sean's chest. "Hey!"

"Ha-ha!" It was Mr. Kruger, holding a small radio controller box. "Rockets sold separately."

Then the man turned to Sean's father and crooked a long finger at him. He shuffled across the floor. "Walk this way, yes?"

"Sure, if I can." Mr. Vickers shuffled after him.

Sean noticed that the toymaker's streak of white hair went all the way back behind his ear to his skin. It ended in a black spot on his neck.

"Ultra creepy," Sean whispered to himself.

"Will you take a look at this!" Mr. Vickers whistled from the backroom. "Now, this is my town! Grover's Mill! I can't believe the detail."

Sean entered the backroom and walked over to a long table. He had to agree, the detail was amazing. One little house even had lights on inside. There was the Double Dunk Donut Den clock and even Lake Lake.

Suddenly the bell on the door jangled and Mrs. Vickers came in carrying a flat white box. The room smelled instantly of pizza with anchovies.

"What *is* that smell?" the toymaker snarled.

"Oh, no!" Mr. Vickers screamed out. "Don't anyone move!" He ran and snatched the white box from his wife and whipped out the steaming hot pizza. "Flying saucer from Pluto!" he screamed. "The fiercest alien force in the galaxy!"

Mr. Vickers flung the cheesy pizza over the model town. It whizzed and almost hovered for a second, just like real flying saucers do.

The horror movie director crouched low and made a frame with his fingers as if he were watching the pizza through a camera.

But then — no! — the cheesy pie started to dip.

"It's not going to make it!" Sean gasped.

The tall toymaker rushed over in horror

as he saw the pizza coming in fast for a landing.

FLOOOOTH!

The crust caught the tip of a tiny water tower and pulled the whole thing down with a crash. A sudden rush of water splashed out on the table.

"Hey! Realistic!" Sean's father cried out in joy.

A big anchovy slapped the side of a little white house above the lake while the rest of the pizza spun to the distant mountains.

"Crash landing!" Mr. Vickers cheered. "Aliens all dead! Another victory for earthlings!" He posed with his hands on his hips.

Mrs. Vickers hummed big movie music.

"Yoooooou!" screamed the tall man, whipping the pizza off his creation. "How could you?"

Mr. Vickers' eyebrows shot up and he smiled like a kid opening presents. "Like this!" He curled his hand toward him then flipped it out, as if he were throwing another pizza. "Wanna try? I can run out and get a small cheese — "

"I AM A GENIUS!" the tall man proclaimed. "My incredible work is too good for you and your horrible movies!"

"*Horror* movies," Mr. Vickers corrected him. He looked at his wife. She smiled and nodded.

"No!" the man gasped. "I've seen them. They're terrible!"

"You mean *terror-filled*?" Mr. Vickers said.

"I mean — bad!" said Mr. Kruger.

"As in *evil*?" Mr. Vickers grinned delightedly. "Yes! I can see we're thinking the same way about my movies. I'll be back in two days to pick up my town!"

Mr. Vickers slipped his arm around his wife's waist, and strode out the door into the street, licking cheese from his fingers.

Sean edged to the back of the room toward a door that was slightly open.

The moment he reached for the door-knob, Mr. Kruger shuffled in front of him. "Forbidden!" he said.

"Eeeee!" a scream suddenly filled the shop.

It was Holly! Sean whirled around just in time to see a furry white cat fly across the room and dive for a piece of little silver fish that had fallen off the flying pizza. Anchovy!

"Fluffy, no!" cried Mr. Kruger. "Not the stinky fish!" The tall man pushed his cat away from the anchovy. The cat flashed its eyes and snarled. Then it jumped on the table and began to slurp up the water from fake Lake Lake.

Mr. Kruger shuffled over to Sean, leaned down, and stared in his face. "You like it here, I can tell." Then he paused and said, "You will be back."

The man said it quietly and simply. As if it were a command.

You will be back.

Then Mr. Kruger rolled his hands over and over as if he was going to pick up a sandwich and bite it.

Sean's tongue got thick. He couldn't say a word. He felt all jittery and nervous again and he didn't like it.

He shoved past Holly and ran out the door.

The Trouble with Things

When they got home Sean leaped right into his swimming trunks. "Going to the pool with Jeff!" he yelled on his way out the door.

When he jumped on his bike, he nearly fell over. The pedals seemed to be too far away.

"Hey, who's been messing with my bike?" he cried. But he was already late. He stood up on the pedals and pushed off down Elm Road.

Sean stopped at the corner of Oak Lane and waited. He looked up and down Birch Street. "Come on, Jeff, we're late," he mumbled.

Sean felt his forehead. It was burning. That's the trouble, he thought, I'm coming down with something. I've got a fever and it's making me feel strange.

He searched the street for a sign of his friend on his bike. "Jeff, you are nowhere on time!"

Finally, Sean saw him. Jeff was leaping over the sidewalk cracks, in red high-tops with blue laces trailing behind. He was holding a towel.

Sean pedaled over. "Where's your bike?"

Jeff trotted to a stop, wiping his forehead. He bent to tie his shoes. "I can't find my bike."

"You can't find it?" Sean asked.

Jeff shrugged. "Well, it was in the garage. My dad's car is gone, too."

"Gone? You mean, stolen?" Sean said.

"I guess," Jeff said. "But whoever took my bike and my dad's car, took the garage, too."

Sean looked at him. "The garage?" He

could see that Jeff was trying to be cheerful, but it wasn't working. He could burst into tears in a second. "Hey, they'll find it. I mean there's probably a special garage squad or something."

"You think?" Jeff asked. "Maybe a team of special guys?"

"Sure. Now hop on," said Sean. "We're late!"

Jeff stepped over the back fender and Sean stood, driving down hard on the pedals.

When they got to Beach Pool right next to Lake Lake, the line for diving lessons was already forming. Mr. Gilman, the school coach who taught swimming over the summer, was standing at the front of the line.

"Hurry, he's got his clipboard!" cried Jeff.

"Not the horrible clipboard!" Sean laughed.

Sean squeezed into line behind Liz Duffey. Liz was okay, but Sean thought she must have done something wacko with her hair. It was really big, In fact, it was like a huge forest towering over him.

"Ryan Jeff," said Mr. Gilman, making a mark on his clipboard. He always called everybody by their last names first, even himself. "I'm Gilman Mister," he said. "Good. Everybody here."

Then the coach said something very strange. "Except Vickers Sean. Vickers not here. Not good."

"Hey, I'm here!" Sean called out. He broke line and waved his arms back and forth. "I'm here."

"Oh," he said. "Stand tall, Vickers. Can't see you if you hide behind Duffey Liz's hair."

Everybody laughed, even Liz and Jeff.

Sean tried to smile but couldn't. What's going on here? he thought.

"Okay, Vickers Sean, front and center," said Mr. Gilman. "Show me how you dive."

Sean walked over to the side of the pool. He tried to get into a good dive position,

but his trunks were bothering him. They seemed a little loose. He hiked them up and twisted his waist. That felt better.

Sean aimed for the ripply blue water.

Mr. Gilman made some squiggles on his clipboard then looked up again. "No, no, Vickers. Trouble with your form. Ryan Jeff, do it with him."

Jeff stepped over, tucked his head between his shoulders, and squatted low. "Like this."

Sean twisted himself to look like Jeff.

"Dive!" Mr. Gilman called out.

The two boys dived together in their twin blue-and-orange racing trunks. They hit the water at the same time. It was warm. It felt great.

They swam over to the side together, slapping the water in unison. As they pulled themselves out of the pool, Mr. Gilman had his head buried in his clipboard.

"Water's warm," Sean said.

A second later, everybody on the other

side of the pool was laughing and pointing into the water. There, in the light and dark ripples on the surface of the water, something was floating. Something orange. With blue stripes.

"What?" Sean grabbed a towel from a chair.

He shot a look at Jeff. Jeff's trunks were tight around him.

Sean ran.

Sean dashed into the pool house rest room and yanked his clothes off the hook. He jumped into his pants and pulled his belt tight. But even the last hole was too loose.

"My clothes are all against me!" he yelped. Finally, he just tied his belt in a knot.

"This is nutzoid!" he mumbled. "Something very weird is going on here."

Sean peeked out the door of the rest room. He'd have to make a break for it. He tore off to the bike stand. He pulled his bike out, and climbed onto the seat.

In the fraction of a second before the

bike tipped over, Sean saw his feet dangle inches above the pedals.

Wham! He fell over onto the grass. His bike tumbled on top of him.

"Whoa!" yelled Jeff, running out of the rest room, pulling his T-shirt over his head. "What's with you and bikes? Did you forget how they work?"

"Not funny!" Sean snapped, getting up again.

Jeff pulled the bike up by its handlebar. "Stand aside. I'll pedal, you ride!"

The laughter still coming from the pool jabbed and jabbed poor Sean's brain like a fork trying to stab peas.

Sean felt as if he were burning up. His cheeks were red-hot.

When they rounded the corner of Maple and Elm, Sean saw his garage door open. "Leave me here, you take the bike."

"What? Hey, wait!" Jeff yelled. But before he could turn around, Sean had disappeared into his garage.

From there, Sean slid into the house,

dashed through the back hall, across the kitchen, and up the stairs without his parents seeing him.

He needed to get to his room. He needed time to think. He needed —

"Ooof!" He collided with Holly coming out of her bedroom.

Their noses nearly touched.

Sean froze. His whole body went icy cold.

Some tiny part of his brain that was still working said, *Holly is four inches shorter than you, Sean. Why is she staring at you, eye to eye? Why is she the same size as you? Why? Why?*

Sean pushed Holly aside, dived into his room, and slammed the door shut.

He stood in front of the mirror and let go of his pants. They fell limp on the floor. The sleeves on his T-shirt dangled to his wrists. The shirt bottom nearly touched the carpet.

What Sean saw in the mirror struck him with such terror that he almost fainted. His body was like a balloon losing air.

Inch by inch, he was getting shorter.

Getting smaller.

Shrinking!

That morning he was nearly five feet tall. But he must have lost almost five inches in the last hour! And it seemed to be going faster!

Sean's whole room seemed to be growing around him. What would happen when he reached four feet? Three feet?

His clothes puffed up around him.

"I'm melting!" he shrieked to himself.

Suddenly, the doorknob turned and the door opened into the room.

"No! Go away!" yelled Sean, backing away behind his desk. But the sound he made was high and whiny. Could anyone even hear that?

The door swung wide.

It was Holly. "Hey, Sean," she started, looking all around the room. "Liz just called and told me what happened to you at the poo — poo — pool — "

She glanced behind the desk.

Sean got hot all over. His tongue felt thick and rubbery, like a school hamburger.

"Get out!" he squeaked. "Get out!"

But she didn't. Holly closed the door, stepped closer, and looked at Sean. He must have been down near two feet now. He could almost stand upright under his desk.

Holly stared at him, her mouth hanging open. "What's *happening* to you?"

Sean couldn't take it. A huge sob welled up in his throat and pushed itself out as if he had swallowed a baseball and his stomach didn't want it there. "I don't know! I'm . . . shrinking! It's stupid. I'm dying or something! It's probably some . . . bad thing."

"What bad thing?" Holly asked.

"I don't know," he sobbed. Terror began to creep into every thought. He couldn't be sure about anything. "Maybe something bad I did."

Holly rolled her eyes. "Dummy! Is your brain shrinking, too?"

Sean gasped. *"Maybe it is!* Maybe my brain *is* shrinking! I'll start to get dumber. Like a little kid. Then a baby. Then a nothing, a zero, a — !"

"Stop it, Sean!" Holly said. "You're shrinking. Okay, it happens. Now let's think about this. Did you eat any strange food?"

Sean wiped his forehead with his huge T-shirt. He was still getting smaller. About a foot and a half, now, he thought. "Well, I had some eyeball candy and washed it down with that blue stuff Dad keeps in the milk carton. And some of that green goo on the counter — "

Holly nodded. "The stuff that looks like pudding but isn't? No, that wouldn't do this."

Sean couldn't see across the top of his bed anymore.

"Did you go anywhere different in the

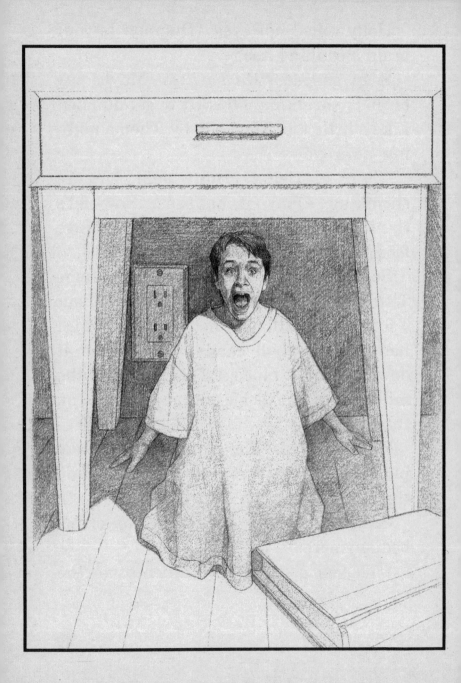

last few days?" Holly asked him. "Something you did that no one else did?"

"The only place was Kruger's Toy World — "

"No, we all went there." Holly shook her head and looked away.

Sean knew he must be gross to look at. He knew he was still getting smaller. But there was something else that kept popping back into his mind. "Kruger was very weird."

"I'll be right back," Holly whispered. She left the room.

Sean wondered how long he would last. He was probably only about a foot tall now, maybe less.

But his mind kept whirling like a hurricane. The toy shop. The tiny Grover's Mill for his dad's movie. Pizza with anchovies. Mr. Kruger. His cat, Fluffy. What did any of this have to do with him shrinking?

A minute later Holly was back with her pocketbook. She took out a bunch of stuff and put it on the floor next to Sean. "I brought these for you. You can change out of your diaper now."

Sean began picking through a pile of tiny blue shorts and weird glittery vests that Holly's "Ron" doll wore. "Oh, man, this is pathetic."

"Don't worry, Ron won't mind." She smiled.

Then Sean stopped. In the pile was something familiar. Jeans and a T-shirt. A W. Reid Elementary School T-shirt! "My clothes! My sneakers, too! This is amazing. How could these clothes — "

Suddenly something struck Sean. Not something heavy, something —

"Light!"

Holly looked up at the ceiling light. "What about the light?"

"No. Last night. When we went biking up to find Mike Mazur's house. And there was the blast of *light*."

"You're sure it wasn't the moon?" Holly asked.

"No! And I was wearing these clothes!" Sean said.

"You can wear them again, it's okay."

"You don't get it," said Sean. "These clothes are the same size as me. They must have been shrinking the same as me! But I only wore this shirt with these pants once — yesterday!"

Then it hit him. Of course! He was the only one who saw the blast. He was the only one who was *in* the blast. "It was the light, the purple light, that made me small!"

Kid Shrinks

"Yes! I remember now," Sean said, jumping into his T-shirt and pants. "The blast of light made me shrink!"

Holly shook her head from side to side slowly. "It's impossible. Things like this don't happen."

"Yeah, don't I wish," Sean said. "Have you forgotten that we live in Weirdsville, USA? Besides, just look at me. I'm the size of a . . . a . . ."

"Toy?" Holly added.

"The toymaker!" Sean squeaked. "He must know something about this. He must! I've got to get there!" Sean started running for the door.

"But what does Mr. Kruger have to do with the purple light you saw?" Holly asked.

Sean stopped. "I don't know — yet. But look, he makes small stuff. I'm small. Not only that, I think he's hiding something in that closet of his. Hey, all I know is I've got to get back to that toy shop. The answer's there!"

Holly stood up. "I'd better tell Mom and Dad about this."

"No!" Sean shouted. "They'll just take me to some hospital and I'd get smaller and smaller and no one would believe me and I'd probably just disappear forever."

Holly bit her lip. "You're right. We need to do something now." She looked him straight in the eye and swallowed hard. "I don't want a little brother. I want a big brother like before."

She unzipped her pocketbook and held it open on the floor. "Get in!"

Sean stepped back. "What?" he sniffed. "I can't fit in there!"

But he could, and it shocked him. He was now no more than four inches tall. The size of a little action figure. The size of a toy.

Taking a deep breath, Sean climbed in Holly's pocketbook, into the middle of a bunch of girl stuff — a comb, a lipstick, a purple puppy pad, a glitter pen, and a mirror.

The mirror was only about four inches long, but Sean could see his whole body. "Thanks. Now I can see just how small I am."

"Hang on," she said. "We're going downstairs to call Jeff. I'll tell him to meet us at the store."

ZIIPPPP! Holly zipped him in. He could feel her lifting the pocketbook and pulling the strap over her shoulder.

Then he felt her bouncing down the stairs. The next thing he knew, she was gently setting the pocketbook down on something. He crawled to the top and peered out.

The kitchen table! His father was there, a bowl of Wheat-O cereal and a cup of coffee in front of him. He was reading the *Grover's Mill Gazette*.

Holly went over to the telephone and dialed a number. Then she stretched the cord from the kitchen to the living room. "Hello, Jeff?"

Mr. Vickers rattled the newspaper and turned the page. Sean read the headlines on the front. "Water Tower Diapers" was on top. Below that was an article called "Doctor Varnishes." Along the side was one called "Sports on Pluto."

Sure, thought Sean. How long would it be before there was a story about him. "Local Boy Shrinks." But no, the *Gazette* always spelled everything wrong, so it would probably be something like "Loco Boy Stinks!"

"Hey, that toymaker!" Mr. Vickers suddenly burst out. "He sure loves my movies! Well, who doesn't love a Humongous Horror Movie?"

"No one, Dad," Holly shouted from the living room.

"Quite right, daughter!" Mr. Vickers said. He set the paper down and placed a Wheat-O on the handle of his cereal spoon. Closing his eyes, he slammed down the other end of the spoon so that the tiny Wheat-O flipped in the air right into his mouth.

Slam! Flip! Slurp! Mmm! Mr. Vickers quickly loaded another Wheat-O.

Sean looked up at the giants around him and a sudden, chilling fear settled over him. His father, even his little sister, could kill him with a single move. Squash him right onto the table. An inch one way or the other and he'd be mushed cookie dough. Then a single wipe of the sponge and he'd be gone!

When no one was looking, Sean slipped out of the pocketbook and onto the table. He ducked behind the coffee cup.

He felt totally alone in a world of giants. Everything he knew was changed. Everything was different now. He wasn't like his family anymore. He was even weirder. He was a freak.

Maybe they'd put him on display.

Sure, thought Sean. Kid Shrinko! Mini Boy! Freak Child! They'd write articles about him. He'd be in books. Even in The Weird Zone he'd be weird! He had to get out of there!

Slam! Flip! Slurp!

Sean panicked. He ran.

Slam! Flip! Slurp!

But he slipped on a drip of coffee and fell over the end of his father's spoon, knocking the next Wheat-O off.

With one quick stroke — *slam!* — Sean was propelled into the air. He was flipping over and over on his way to his father's open mouth!

Stomp That Boy!

The wet tongue! The saliva! The sharp teeth!

"Yuuuuuck!" screeched tiny Sean as the giant jaws swung open for their treat.

Suddenly Holly was in the air, diving in from the living room, sliding across the kitchen table, her hands stretching for the tiny figure that was not a tasty Wheat-O but Sean Vickers, mini human boy! Her brother!

Wump! She grabbed Sean and tumbled, hitting the floor with a thud.

"Would you like your own bowl of tasty Wheat-O's, dear?" Mr. Vickers asked her.

"I . . . uh." Holly got up and quickly slid Sean into her pocketbook once more. "Dad, can we go to Kruger's Toy World?"

"But my set won't be ready until tomorrow," her father said.

Holly shifted her weight. "I need to get something for Sean's birthday right away."

Mr. Vickers raised an eyebrow and stepped over to the calendar tacked on the wall. "Your brother's birthday is seven months away."

"He's my only brother, Dad," Holly said.

Sean knew how much his sister probably wanted to gag.

"I need to — you know — get him something."

There was a tone in Holly's voice that Sean hadn't heard before. Was it *fear*?

"What children I have!" Mr. Vickers exclaimed. "Grab your pocketbook, missy!"

"I have it," she said, swinging the pocketbook up for him to see.

Sean slid down the puppy pad, getting

his feet stuck in the coil. "Hey, be careful!" he yelled.

After a short ride to Kruger's Toy World, Holly jumped out of the car. She was holding her pocketbook close to her. "Hurry, Dad. Every second counts!"

Sean stuck his head out of the pocketbook.

Suddenly —

Bong! The giant donut-shaped clock on top of the Double Dunk Donut Den struck noon!

Sssss! The enormous pancake pan atop Usher's House of Pancakes also hissed out the hour.

Noon! Lunch! Food time!

An instant later, the sidewalks were a mad rush of flip-flops, sneakers, sandals, and bare feet tearing off toward noontime eats!

Stomp! Stomp! Stomp!

Holly leaped from the sidewalk to avoid a horde of hungry people!

Her pocketbook whipped around behind her.

"Holleeeeeeee!" came the scream.

But she didn't hear.

She walked quickly to the store — as Sean fell, fell, fell, to the stomped-on sidewalk below!

8

Getting Incredible!

"Ooof!" Sean slammed face first onto a little patch of grass right next to the sidewalk.

Suddenly, the ground began to thunder. With each thump Sean was knocked back on his face. He finally managed to turn over.

It was a kid, a huge kid, thumping along the grass with giant sneakers!

"No!" Sean squeaked. "He'll crush me!"

But before he could move, the sky went dark above him. A huge high-top closed in on him! It thundered down on the grass a half inch from his head.

That's when Sean saw that the sneaker

was a red high-top! With blue laces!

"Jeff!" Sean cried out. "Don't squish me!"

But his giant friend didn't hear him. In a moment that sneaker would plant him like a seed!

Sean saw his only chance. Jeff was heading for the toy store. He had to make a move. He rolled over, reached up, and leaped for the blue laces.

Yes! He got one!

He held tight, as the giant shoe lifted, swung quickly up through the air, and took him with it.

Thump! Thump! Thump! Jeff ran over to the toy store's front door. With one powerful swing, he leaped up the step and into the store.

"Now I'm getting somewhere!" Sean said.

But at that moment the big blue laces whipped around.

"Nooo!" Sean lost his grip. He flew up into the air and landed on the soft toe of Jeff's other sneaker.

KA-BOOM! Sean got blasted across the floor of the shop and into a pile of stuffed bears. He crumpled to the floor like a bean-bag. "Oh, this hurts!"

Mr. Kruger looked up from the minia-ture set. He stood and stepped in front of Holly, Jeff, and Mr. Vickers. "I have not yet completed my work!" he growled.

Holly sidestepped him and went straight for the closet in the back. She tried the door.

"That room is locked," Mr. Kruger said, his crooked face beginning to get more crooked. Fluffy the cat jumped up into his arms.

"There's something in that closet Sean and I need to see." Then Holly carefully emptied her purse onto the model town. Lipstick, the purple puppy pad, glitter pen, comb, mirror, all tumbled out into the parking lot of the miniature Plan Nine Drive-in. "Oh, no!" Holly screamed. "Sean's not here!"

"I'm over here!" yelled Sean from across the room. But no one heard.

Mr. Vickers frowned. "I don't think Sean would fit in your pocketbook."

"He would, Dad, he would!" Holly blurted out. "Sean's in trouble — he's tiny! And somehow it's because of this man!"

"Ah, children," the tall man snarled. "Such imagination! Now, if you'll excuse me, I must — "

"But it's true, Mr. V.," added Jeff. "I saw Sean. He is getting little! By now he's probably super small. It's totally — amazing!"

Mr. Vickers' forehead wrinkled. "Excuse me, Jeff. If my son is tiny, he is *incredible*, not *amazing*. We in the movie business always use the word *incredible* to describe extreme smallness. And *amazing* is for big, oversize, colossal — something of that nature. Take, for instance, my new film, *The Amazing* — "

"Dad!" Holly interrupted. "Sean is in trouble!"

"Oh," Mr. Vickers said. "Right!"

But the toymaker pushed them all toward the front door. "The store is *closed*. I must get back to my work."

Sean had to get their attention. If no one could hear him, at least maybe they would see him. He ran out to the middle of the floor. He began to jump up and down.

Suddenly — *meooow!*

Fluffy snarled and leaped from the toymaker's arms. She shot across the room at Sean.

"No!" cried Holly. "No, Fluffy!"

Sean scrambled across the floor and skittered toward the dark closet at the back of the store. He scraped his shoulder as he slid past the underside of the door.

Meooow! Fluffy slammed into the door, but couldn't get in.

In the dim light, Sean saw an enormous dark shape filling the small room.

"You must leave. Now!" he heard Mr. Kruger saying.

"No!" shouted Holly. "Sean needs me!"

But Kruger insisted. A moment later the

shop bell jangled and all was quiet.

Ka-flang! The sound of a bolt sliding shut.

Footsteps slowly stepping across the floor.

"Fluffy, go!" the toymaker growled. The sound of paws scampering away from the door.

Then the closet door opened wide. And Mr. Kruger looked down at Sean. The man's giant crooked face screwed up into a wide and devilish half-grin.

"Is he a boy, or is he a toy?" Kruger said as he took off his thick glasses and pushed his hair back. "Now, we will find out!"

"You can't do this!" Sean cried out. "I'm a kid, a Grover's Mill kid, an American! Let me go!"

No answer from the man with the crooked face. Only laughter. Sinister, horrible, awful, terrifying laughter. It filled the shop.

Sean knew the tall man with the white stripe in his hair didn't want to chitchat. In fact, the man lunged at Sean. He picked him right off the floor, and set him down in the middle of Main Street in little Grover's Mill. "So! My town now has people in it!" he said.

The ground beneath Sean was made of

colored sandpaper. The ceiling was painted blue, like the sky. All around were tiny cardboard buildings. "I don't think I like this," he mumbled.

Suddenly, there was a blur of white.

White fur!

"Oh, dear!" the toymaker snorted, his nostrils flaring with evil delight. "Fluffy has gotten away! Too bad for the little troublemaking boy! Let's see what he does."

"What the boy does is — run!" Sean screamed. He blasted down the sandpaper Main Street. The table rumbled from the galloping paws of the giant cat charging after him!

Sean hung a tight left between two plastic houses and skittered to a stop.

It looked like a garage.

It *really* looked like a garage.

In fact, it *was* a garage!

Jeff Ryan's garage!

And there was a real car in it. And —

"Jeff's bike! This is amaz — I mean, incredible!"

Meooow! A giant cat claw pushed between the houses and swiped at Sean.

Sean ducked, but with that single swat, Fluffy destroyed Jeff's garage.

"Whoa! Mean kitty!" Sean grabbed Jeff's bike and tore off down fake Birch Street. He backtracked quickly and skidded out to Elm Road.

Fluffy leaped over Duffey's Diner in front of the X-Rays Я Us Medical Clinic. She swatted at the sign and knocked down the backward R.

"Ha-ha!" laughed the evil Kruger.

Sean hunched low and powered under the huge furry legs that straddled Maple Drive. He tore out onto Main Street again.

He pumped as fast as he could past the fish-shaped Baits Motel, the WYRD radio tower, and the Double Dunk Donut Den. He veered right at Usher's House of Pancakes.

Everything was fake. The windows were painted on. The doors didn't open. Every-

thing was made of cardboard. "No place to hide!"

Meooow! Fluffy pounced after the tiny shape.

Then, the white killer cat slid to a stop. It spied the fake Lake Lake and scampered over to slurp a drink.

"Thank you!" gasped Sean, as he pedaled up the little bluff overlooking the lake. There was one small white house at the top. He pumped as fast as he could. He was out of breath. But he had to keep going. Faster! Faster!

Sean's wheels spun in the fake dirt.

What he saw then shocked him like a bolt of lightning straight to his brain.

The little white house. It wasn't fake. It wasn't made of plastic.

Sean dropped the bike and ran up to the house.

He tried the door.

It opened.

Zem?

Sean stepped into a living room with furniture. A real living room, with real furniture.

Then he heard it. A tiny sound. A song. And the words!

Camp Smiley — where kids smile.
We smile — in single file.
If it's sunny — or if it's damp,
We smile — when we think of Camp . . .
Smiley!

Sean knew that hearing the Camp Smiley theme song meant only one thing! Someone was singing!

"Hey! Who's here?" he cried out.

The singing stopped. "Sean?" came a voice. There was a rustling sound from another room. Then a boy appeared.

"Mike?" asked Sean. "Mike Mazur?"

"Yeah!" the boy answered, his face brightening. He ran up to Sean and practically hugged him. "Oh, wow! I thought I was all alone here. This is great!"

Sean made a face. "No offense, Mike, but I'd rather be doing chores." He looked around the room. "So, this is your house?"

"Yeah," said Mike. "I got shrunk yesterday I think. There was a flash of — "

"Purple light!" gasped Sean.

"Yeah," said Mike. "How did you know?"

"I was there," Sean said. "I was trying to find your house. Then I got blasted, too. But where are your parents?"

"They were out walking our dog, Spot. They work at the Welles Observatory, so they look up at the sky a lot. They probably didn't notice what happened."

Sean nodded. "Parents. Kind of weird,

aren't they?" He glanced out the living room window. The white cat was licking his paws on the fake beach of Lake Lake. "Fluffy's still busy. That will give us time to think."

"While we shrink," Mike added.

Sean turned to Mike. "Not funny." Then horror jabbed him as he realized his Camp Smiley friend wasn't joking. Mike was still getting smaller. He was still shrinking!

"Mike! You're — " Sean started to say.

"I know. I was in the center of the blast, remember? But you might keep shrinking, too," Mike said. "The only way to stop it is to eat." He rubbed his stomach. "But all the food's gone."

"Maybe some of the stuff we learned at Camp Smiley can help us now," said Sean.

"The great songs?" Mike asked.

"No! Survival stuff," Sean said. "Like eating bark and roots."

Mike made a face. "Everything here is made out of plastic or cardboard."

Sean peered out a side window and saw

Mr. Kruger open the door in the back of the shop. He dragged a big thing out to the center of the room. Whatever the thing was, it was covered with a cloth.

"I don't know what's going on here," said Sean. "But I'm pretty sure it's not good. I'm also pretty sure we're running out of time."

"We're running out of me, too!" Mike added.

Crash! A huge furry white paw suddenly burst through the Mazurs' front window.

Meooow!

"Let's get out of here!" Sean tore across the room toward the back hall. He tripped over a pile of newspapers in the hall and slid on a slimy gooey mess of stinky gray glop.

"What's this?" cried Sean, holding his nose.

"Some kind of alien poison, I think," said Mike. "A flying saucer flew over before and dropped it on my house!"

Sean looked down. It was all over his

sneakers. "Pizza! My dad tossed a pizza and some of it hit your house. These are anchovies! We can eat this stuff! It's fish!"

Mike pulled away. "I'd rather be small."

Meooow! Fluffy was breaking through the front of the house.

"Hey!" cried Sean. "Cats love stinky fish!" He quickly scraped some gray glop onto a newspaper. He opened the back door and flung the mess across the backyard. "Here, kitty, kitty!"

Instantly, Fluffy leaped over the house and dived for the anchovy. She teetered on the edge of the table for a moment, then jumped to the floor with the fish.

"Yes!" cried Sean. "A victory for earthlings!"

"Pah!" boomed the terrible toymaker as his cat dragged the fishy thing across the floor. "Anchovies! I hate zem!"

Sean turned back into the kitchen. *"Zem?"* he said. "What's with his different voice?" He stopped in shock to see a tiny figure scurry across the floor. "Mike!"

His Camp Smiley friend was getting tinier! And Mike was jumping up and down on a newspaper. Sean looked at the paper. It was the same one his father had been reading at breakfast. Instantly, the misspelled headlines made sense.

"Mike, look! 'Water Tower Diapers.' They mean *Disappears*. The Grover's Mill water tower disappeared the other night. And suddenly Kruger has one just like it, with real water!"

"Like my house — " Mike called out.

"And look at this one! 'Doctor Varnishes.' They mean *Vanishes*. Someone named Dr. Gruker vanished from the top secret base in the mountains the very same night."

"My mom told me a lot of weirdos work up there," Mike added.

Sean read more of the newspaper. "It says the guy went crazy making things small, and that he plans to take over the world! It says he's dangerous, and that — " Suddenly Sean gasped. "Wait! *Gruker* is *Kruger* spelled backward!"

Mike frowned. "Well, um, actually, it's not. Gruker is . . . *Rekurg* spelled backward."

"Sideways, then!" cried Sean. "It's him! The toymaker and the weirdo! They're the same!"

"But the paper says Gruker speaks with an accent," said Mike. "Mr. Kruger doesn't speak — "

CRUNNNNCH!

The roof of the little white house was suddenly pulled completely off and the giant crooked face peered down at the two boys.

"Zo!" boomed the voice above them. "Zee leetle boys have discovered my tiny zecret! Velcome!"

"Velcome?" said Mike, curling his lip.

"The accent!" screeched Sean. "He's *Gruker*! He's the weirdo who wants to shrink the world!"

"QUIET ON ZEE SET!" boomed the strange toymaker. He had a small silver box in his hand. "You boys live in a movie

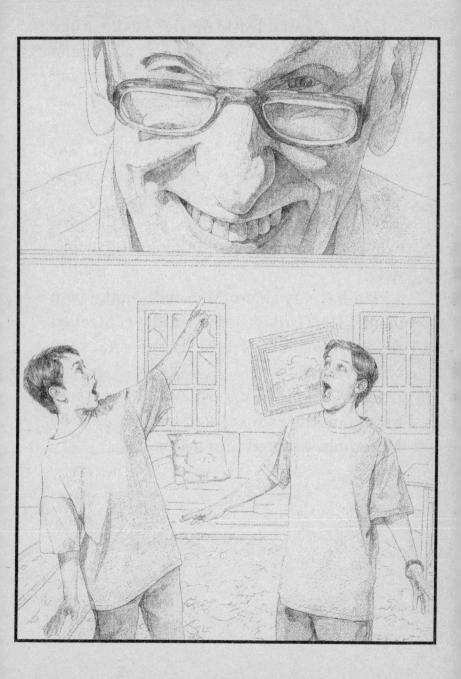

set. How about a leetle movie? I call zis one
— *Attack of zee Moto-Men on zee Leetle
Boys*. I've fiddled with zee controls zo my
Moto-Men just vant to destroy. Does zat
sound good to you?"

"No!" yelled Mike, "*zat* — I mean *that*
doesn't sound good to us!" Mike was getting small, but he was still fierce.

Sean took heart from the little guy.
"Yeah! Make us big! Make us big right
now!"

"Ha-ha! My Moto-Men vill make you
dead!" Dr. Gruker set six radio-controlled
figures on Main Street. "Scene one, take
one. Action!"

Then he smiled his evil smile, pressed a
button on the radio controller box, and the
Moto-Men whirred into action!

Attack of the Moto-Men!

Vrrrrr-CHUNG! KA-CHUNG!

Two smoking rocket bombs spiraled down from the end of mini Main Street and — *BLAM! BLAM!* — burst at the boys' heels!

"Whoa! Toys with an attitude!" shouted Mike, diving behind Sean's sneakers.

"I'd hate to see them in a bad mood!" cried Sean.

The radio-controlled army of metallic Moto-Men lurched forward.

Sean snatched Mike up off the ground and slipped him in his pants pocket. "Mike, we've got to give this the old Camp Smiley try!"

Mike nodded and began to hum the camp song. But there was another song, more horrible, more menacing than Sean had ever heard before.

It screeched and buzzed and whined from the tiny speakers of the advancing army! It went —

> *Singing Moto-Men!*
> *Inches tall, we're ten!*
> *We have rocket arms*
> *And five unique alarms!*
> *Zzz! Vrrr! Eeee! Klang! Wooo!*

Dr. Gruker stood back and scanned the scene below. "Ha-ha! I vill conquer zee vorld! Starting here in Grover's Mill! Starting viss you boys!"

KLA-BAM! Another Moto rocket blasted near the boys, missed, and took the big fish head off the Baits Motel.

Sean dived away from flying bits of cardboard and dashed down Main Street. He wondered if he'd ever see his full-size town again. Sure it was Weirdo's Mill. But it was home.

BLAM! Acme Hardware and Books blew into a thousand tiny pieces of plastic and paper.

> *Perfect gifts to give!*
> *No birthday kid will live!*

"Oh, man!" snorted Mike. "I sure hope their sense of smell is as bad as their words. That fish gunk on your shoes is making me sick!"

It was pretty bad, but still Sean ran. Past Jabba's Diet Center.

"First I shrank a vater tower," Dr. Gruker was saying, beaming as he pushed the big covered shape into the middle of the shop. "Zen a leetle vite house!"

"My house!" Mike snarled from Sean's pocket.

"And zen a garage!" Dr. Gruker said.

"Can't we shut him up?" Mike said in his tiny voice.

"He won't stop," huffed Sean, gasping under the awning of Picard's Hair Salon.

KLA-BLAM! Another Moto rocket blasted behind Sean. "His dumb robots won't stop, either!"

"Zoon, I vill have zis silly town in zee palm of my hand!" Gruker boomed, suddenly whipping the dark cloth off the big thing.

Before him stood a strange and complicated machine on a stand. It nearly reached the ceiling and was cluttered with levers and buttons. At the top was a long barrel with tubes and wires coiling up and down.

"Ach! My amazink shrinkink gun!" Dr. Gruker snarled. "Zee professional toymaker model!"

He positioned the big gun near the front of the shop. "I vill stomp zis leetle town!"

"Hey!" said Sean. "That's my dad's idea!"

"And zen — zee entire vorld shall be mine!"

Suddenly, everything made sense to Sean.

"Mike," he cried, "this guy is a total maniac! We have to stop him before he zaps somebody else!" Sean glanced toward the miniature Plan Nine Drive-in. "I'm going to try something. It's pretty crazy. It's mega wild."

"What if it doesn't work?" cried Mike. "What if we can't stop him?"

"It has to work! Besides, all the nutzoids in my dad's horror movies get stopped."

"Unless there's a sequel," Mike squeaked.

"You would have to say that!" Sean grumbled. "Now come with me!"

"Where else would I go? I'm in your pocket."

Mike was in Sean's pocket, all right. But just barely. He felt to Sean like a wisp with hardly any weight at all. Sean was getting smaller, too.

We love to terminate!
And yes, exterminate!

"Hurry!" yelped Mike. "It's the Motor-Mouth-Men!"

VRRRR — BLAM! A huge explosion plowed the corner of Elm Road, and Sean's own cardboard house blew up in pieces!

Sean darted over a nearby wall and into the parking lot of the Plan Nine Drive-in. "Sheesh! *Zis* guy *vants* us dead!"

Mike peered up at huge Sean. "And *zat's* not good!" He almost smiled.

Sean raced over to the middle of the parking lot. A pile of big stuff was sitting there. A giant comb, a lipstick, a mirror, a purple puppy pad, a glitter pen. Everything that Holly had dumped from her purse. Sean grabbed the pencil and dragged it over near the wall.

Then he went back for the mirror and pulled it over the pencil like a seesaw.

"Um, now is not the time to play, Sean!"

Mike said, his voice getting tinier and tinier.

"It's an old trick my dad taught me," Sean said. "Now comes the crazy part."

Sean climbed the wall and waved. "Hey, Moto-Morons! Over here! Yoo-hoo, Meat-o Heads!"

That did the trick. The Moto-Men immediately jerked over to the Drive-in. Sean jumped down and crouched on one end of the mirror.

WHIRRR! One Moto-Man climbed up to the top of the wall, towering over tiny Sean.

"Exterminate!" it sang.

Sean jammed his thumbs in his ears and stuck out his tongue. "You have a lousy voice!"

The giant blue metal Moto-Man began to jiggle. Its eyes flashed red sparks.

"So, toys have feelings, too!" said Mike.

The Moto-Man leaped in robotic anger at the boys and landed right on the seesaw mirror.

BOING! The boys went flying!

Yes! It worked! The old "Wheat-O on the spoon" trick!

But — oh, no! — the force was too great!

The mirror shot up, hit the ceiling, and fell at the exact same time that Sean went blasting feetfirst across the shop!

Suddenly, a face appeared at the shop door. Gruker hunched over the horrible machine. His nose flared wide with evil delight. "Good! More tiny leetle peep — peep — *pooooth!*"

Sean's stinky feet shot like bullets directly into the evil man's nostrils!

One in each.

Gruker's nose exploded in a huge snort. "I hate anchovies!"

But it was too late! The evil toymaker's evil hand had already hit the evil switch.

Holly came bursting through the door, just as the room exploded in a blast of purple light!

The Zone That's Weird

Zing! Zing! Zing! BLAMMO!

Holly's little mirror tumbled down in front of the shrinking gun at the exact instant the ray went off.

"Ooof!" gasped Sean, still in midair.

"Ooof!" gasped Mike, squished in his pocket.

"Ooof!" gasped Dr. Gruker, doubling over onto the floor.

Smoke instantly filled the air.

Sean crashed against a bunch of stuff and landed back in the middle of Main Street.

He looked through the smoke and saw two figures jump up and run over to him.

It was Holly and Jeff. Their footsteps echoed off the sides of the buildings.

"Oh, no!" cried Sean. "Not you, too!"

Holly ran closer. "Sean, are you all right?"

Sean stood up and dusted himself off. "Yeah, but, you guys. Man, I'm sorry. You're — "

"That blast almost destroyed the whole shop," said Jeff.

"What?" asked Sean. Then, as the smoke cleared, Sean noticed something different about Main Street. It wasn't made of sandpaper.

He looked up. And there was sky over him! Real sky. Not a painted blue ceiling.

He whirled around. There was the toy shop behind him, smoke streaming from the windows and door.

"Hey! This isn't miniature Grover's Mill," gasped Sean. "It's real Grover's Mill! Filled with real people! And I'm big again!"

Sean hugged his sister and jumped up and down on Main Street. On Main Street in the exact center of intergalactic weirdness. "Holly! Holly! Your mirror — it worked! It reversed the shrinking ray. I'm big again!"

Then he stopped. "Wait. Where's Mike?" Sean started for the store. "Mike? Mike!"

A sudden pain hit his stomach. "Ooof!" He doubled over. Something was happening to him. He felt weird. "Oh, no! Not again!"

KRIPPPPP!

Sean's pocket tore open and full-sized Mike Mazur came blasting out into the dirt.

Holly stood back. "That was weird."

Jeff ran over and helped Mike up. "You must be Mike Mazur, the new kid."

"Um, I think so." Mike smiled a little smile and dusted off his shirt. "Nice town you've got here."

Holly laughed. "Welcome to The Weird Zone."

A dreadful cry suddenly ripped through

the smoky air. "I'm shrinking! I'M SHRINKING!"

"That wasn't me, was it?" Sean gasped.

The voice was coming from inside the smoldering ruins of the toy shop. It squeaked and squealed like a balloon losing air.

The voice belonged to Dr. Gruker!

Sean, Holly, Jeff, and Mike ran into the shop, fanning away the smoke.

Finally, they spotted a tiny figure running across the floor. It had a streak of white in its black hair. It was getting smaller and smaller.

WOOO-EEE-OOO-EEE!

Sirens wailed from outside. The kids ran out to see trucks and ambulances and tanks and jeeps come roaring in from the secret army base north of town.

THONKA-THONKA-THONKA!

A giant helicopter swept over Main Street. Jeff Ryan's mother jumped out of the swirling tornado of wind and dust. She was dressed in a military uniform. She motioned, and special troops in black uniforms swarmed into the toy shop.

A few minutes later a bunch of soldiers came out of the smoky shop holding a little box.

Mrs. Ryan patted Sean and Mike on their backs. "I see the good doctor got a taste of his own bitter medicine." She examined the box. Inside was a mini Dr. Gruker. He shook a tiny fist at Sean. "I vill get you for zis!" he whined.

"Strange," Mrs. Ryan said, as the soldiers took the doctor away. "All this time we've been searching for a man named *Gruker*. So clever of him to change his name to Kruger! The ultimate disguise!"

The kids nodded.

Beep-beep! Mrs. Ryan reached for a little device on her belt and put it up to her ear. She listened for a moment then snapped the device back on her belt. "Sorry, kids. I can't stay. There's a report of an enormous white cat over at Lake Lake. Cats that big don't exist, of course, but we have to check it out."

She turned to one of the special troops. "Giant mew-mew at Lake Lake!"

THONKA! THONKA!

A moment later she was gone.

As Sean looked out his own living room window, the orangey-brown desert spread away as far as the eye could see. "Nice to be big again."

He turned to his family gathered with him. "It's amazing what we've just been through. Like one of your movies, Dad."

"Yes," agreed Mr. Vickers. "I'm only disappointed I didn't get any of your little adventure on film. Ah, well. Perhaps next time."

Sean made a face. "Next time?"

"Truly we're delighted you're normal size again, honey," Mrs. Vickers said, walking in from the kitchen with a plate of little sandwiches and other party treats. "Although having a tiny son could be quite handy for getting into those hard-to-clean spots!"

Sean made another face.

"Hey, shrimp!" said a voice behind him.

Sean went icy cold. "Not again!" A drop of sweat dripped down his neck as he whirled around.

There was Holly, smiling up at him. In her hands was a plate of little pink shrimps and dipping sauce. "Shrimp, big brother. Have one."

Sean laughed. "What? No anchovies?"

"You kids get snug for the video," said Sean's mother. "I'll get my *special* dip." She laughed and hummed a jazzy tune on her way to the kitchen. Mr. Vickers twisted the ends of a mustache that wasn't there and swept after her.

"It's amazing being normal again," Sean murmured. "And it was your mirror that did the trick. It reversed the shrinking ray.

Mike's house is back by the lake. Jeff's garage is where it's supposed to be. And I got big."

"But not too big," Holly added. "Just somewhere between incredible and amazing."

"Hey, I like that." Sean smiled and sat next to Holly on the couch as the TV lit up. A news report was in progress. A reporter was holding a microphone up to Jeff Ryan's mother.

" . . . we finally subdued the giant cat," Mrs. Ryan was saying, "after it nearly choked on a pair of swimming trunks floating in the pool . . ."

Sean was quiet for a while. Then he turned to Holly. "Pretty weird day, huh?"

Mr. and Mrs. Vickers danced into the room.

A bolt of green lightning flashed in the sky.

Something rumbled deep below the ground.

Holly shrugged. "Kind of like every day around here."

She clicked the VCR remote and the screen went red with the title of their dad's latest horror movie, *Worm Man vs. the Human Gadget!*

Scary music began to play.

Sean felt all warm inside. All snug. Yeah, he thought. Kind of like every day in The Weird Zone.

Bong! went the donut clock.

Sssss! went the pancake pan.

THE LEFTOVERS #3:

USE THEIR HEADS!

by Tristan Howard

GOOOOAL!
Baseball season is over, and the Rangers are
now a soccer team. Will they be any better at
soccer than they were at baseball?
Only if they remember to use their heads,
not their hands!

COMING IN AUGUST 1996!

L01195

The Adventures of THE BAILEY SCHOOL KIDS™

Frankenstein Doesn't Plant Petunias, Ghosts Don't Eat Potato Chips, and Aliens Don't Wear Braces ... or do they?

Find out about the creepiest, weirdest, funniest things that happen to The Bailey School Kids!™ Collect and read them all!

❏ BAS47070-1	Aliens Don't Wear Braces	$2.99
❏ BAS48114-2	Cupid Doesn't Flip Hamburgers	$2.99
❏ BAS22638-X	Dracula Doesn't Drink Lemonade	$2.99
❏ BAS22637-1	Elves Don't Wear Hard Hats	$2.99
❏ BAS47071-X	Frankenstein Doesn't Plant Petunias	$2.99
❏ BAS50961-6	Gargoyles Don't Drive School Buses	$2.99
❏ BAS47297-6	Genies Don't Ride Bicycles	$2.99
❏ BAS45854-X	Ghosts Don't Eat Potato Chips	$2.99
❏ BAS48115-0	Gremlins Don't Chew Bubblegum	$2.99
❏ BAS44822-6	Leprechauns Don't Play Basketball	$2.99
❏ BAS50960-8	Martians Don't Take Temperatures	$2.99
❏ BAS22635-5	Monsters Monsters Don't Scuba Dive	$2.99
❏ BAS22639-8	Mummies Don't Coach Softball	$2.99
❏ BAS47298-4	Pirates Don't Wear Pink Sunglasses	$2.99
❏ BAS44477-8	Santa Claus Doesn't Mop Floors	$2.99
❏ BAS48113-4	Skeletons Don't Play Tubas	$2.99
❏ BAS43411-X	Vampires Don't Wear Polka Dots	$2.99
❏ BAS44061-6	Werewolves Don't Go to Summer Camp	$2.99
❏ BAS48112-6	Witches Don't Do Backflips	$2.99
❏ BAS50962-4	Wizards Don't Need Computers	$2.99
❏ BAS22636-3	Zombies Don't Play Soccer	$2.99
❏ BAS88134-5	Bailey School Kids Special Edition #1 Mrs. Jeepers Is Missing	$4.99

Available wherever you buy books, or use this order form